Faithful Love

Believe in one another

By R.K. Amber

ISBN: 0-578-47753-X
ISBN-13: 978-0-578-47753-4

DEDICATION

I dedicate this book to my lovely wife Amber. Thank you for your support and being the love of my life and my best friend.

CONTENTS

ACKNOWLEDGMENTS

I would like to thank my wife Amber for helping me review and read the many revisions of this short story with powerful thoughtfulness and kindness. I would like to thank my friend Dave who helped bring this short story to life with his beautifully creative and colorful illustrations. Lastly, I want to thank my sister, my mom and my friends for your encouragement and support.

BLAKE

Late into my third year of marriage, I attended my fifteen-year high school reunion. My wife had come down with the flu just days before, so she'd insisted that I attend the ceremony without her.

I made the trip from Seattle to Chicago alone, and honestly, I think I needed the trip. I needed a break from her. The last few weeks with her had been stressful: She no longer found my corny jokes amusing, she didn't eat when I cooked for her, and we didn't make love anymore. I didn't think she was attracted to me anymore, but I wasn't rushing to any conclusions. I thought it might be some type of midlife crisis that would pass. I just needed to be patient with her.

The reunion was held in our high school gymnasium. The music was blaring and intensified slowly as I approached the gym. Inside was colorful. There were excessively bright lights, and our high school pictures decorated the hallway. Because this was my first time attending a reunion of any kind, I hadn't been sure how to dress, so I'd kept it semiformal. I wore a grey dress shirt with my go-to striped tie and my black pair of shoes.

Nostalgia engulfed me soon after I walked in. I remembered the days I'd spent in detention, I remembered the time I'd toilet-papered Ryan Green's locker because he had bullied me occasionally, and I remembered my first kiss. It had been with Alice Kennedy, the head cheerleader, who'd kissed me right in front of my locker with everybody staring; it had been part of some dare by her friends. For the next few days, I'd been the most talked-about topic in school.

I was not the coolest kid in high school, but I was not the geekiest either. I found the balance between cool and geeky, and I got along with everybody. As a result, I had no clique and no friends. I was a loner . . . no, not the type you would feel pity for and then eat lunch with because you wanted him to have some company for the first time; I was the cool kind. I was the guy who ate lunch with Mr. Kaplan, our geography teacher, because I didn't want to be in the spotlight nor have any friends or mortal enemies. I had mastered the nods of the jocks, the right words to say to the Goths, the right language to use when talking to the theater folk, the best tone to use in conversations with the stoners, and the walk to use when passing by the rich kids.

The days after the Alice Kennedy kiss were weird. Suddenly, the spotlight had been shone on me: People watched everything I did, who I hung out with, who I ate with, and who I sat with. They soon realized that I was a loner, and the spotlight was taken from me; I was not worthy of it. I was no longer the cool loner; I was just a loner. I think Alice Kennedy genuinely liked me, but her kind and mine were not meant to get along. It would defy the rules of her social hierarchy and obliterate the coveted social strata. Besides, if she did hang out with me, the geeks would think they had a chance with the jocks, and then the Goths would believe they were not the odd ones and that we were the odd ones. The whole school would be in shambles. So, I understood her inhibitions. But the taste of her lips on mine lingered as I walked past my old locker.

I waited at the entrance to the gym. The sight of these people suddenly made me sick. I realized that I'd never liked them; they'd never been my friends. John Ridgewell saw me standing at the entrance to the gym and dragged me inside.
"Hey, Blake! How are you doing?"
I mumbled a response, and the next minute, I found myself doing shots with John and his friends.

JENNIFER

I awoke to the faint smell of his cologne, and I suddenly missed him. I wished I hadn't been such an ass to him when he'd woken me to inform me of his departure. I grabbed the sheets, hoping to get a whiff of whatever piece of him he had left behind. I was down with the flu, but I could function properly. It was mild, but I had overplayed it because I hadn't wanted to go with him to the stupid reunion and meet his friends and high school girlfriends. I hadn't wanted to be his trophy wife. I hadn't wanted to be the one he would present to his friends to show that he had lucked out in the wife lottery. I told myself these things, but the real reason I hadn't wanted to go was that I didn't think I could pretend that all was well with us, especially under that level of scrutiny.

I could keep up appearances with my parents and the neighbors, but not in a room filled with strangers who would ask piercing questions, such as "What is Blake really like these days? He was like the coolest kid in high school" or "Does Blake still tell jokes? He was a total comedian in high school." Or perhaps a high school girlfriend would ask something like "Is he still a passionate lover? Blake is the most passionate lover I've ever had!" I knew that this wasn't how these things worked, but this was how I'd imagined them to. I blamed the Hollywood movies for their portrayal of high school reunions, and this was why I hadn't gone to any of mine.

I wished Blake would have just understood that I'd played sick because I hadn't wanted him to go to the stupid high school reunion. But I didn't blame him either. These past few weeks, I'd been nothing but a pain in the ass to him. I stayed home in bed all day with our cat, Fluffy, and binge-watched TV shows.

Marie Ann, my colleague from work, had come by earlier to check on me, and although it had been a really nice gesture, I'd hated that she'd come. I'd had to pretend that I'd been really sick, and she'd kept asking these annoying questions about Blake that I hadn't wanted answer. He had been on my mind since he'd left, and the second, I'd found something to distract me from thinking about him, Marie Ann had stepped in and reminded me of him throughout her visit. She'd kept saying stuff such as "You shouldn't have let him go on that trip, Jen. High school reunions are basically bacchanalian. They are filled with slutty exes, excessive alcohol, and overzealous friends who do nothing but remind you of your high school years and advise you to live in the moment." When I'd keep quiet instead of replying to her, she'd continued. "We both know these things have one thing written all over them—bad decisions. Don't you remember the Hollywood Movie *40 and Counting* that we went to see last girls' night out? Remember how someone got pregnant at the reunion?"

"Blake is not like that, and his high school reunion is nothing like that movie," I'd said with a carefree attitude. But now, I really couldn't help thinking that she might be right; Marie Ann was never wrong about these things. She was the one who'd told Joanne in marketing that her husband had a mistress, and this had been months before Joanne had found out. Marie Ann had even found out that her own husband had fathered a kid with another woman eight months before he'd come clean and told her about it. She had a hunch for things of this nature; it was like her hidden talent.

Marie Ann had left at a little after 2 pm. I had been aching to call Blake, but I hadn't wanted to do it in front of her, as I hadn't wanted her to think that her words had made me uneasy or that I did not trust my husband.

I picked up my phone and attempted to dial, but I didn't want to come across as the nagging wife who wouldn't let her husband have a night out with his friends. He actually never called me during my girls' nights out to quiz me about what we were doing and with whom. I felt bad that my trust in him had wavered. I needed to clear my head; I was no longer thinking straight. And how could I doubt Blake, who had not even looked twice at a woman since we'd started dating back in college? When had I become the obnoxious wife?

4

I changed into my running gear; a run would clear my head. My hair was a complete mess and the usual color; greyish with a blend of brown. I stepped out a little after Marie Ann had left and the atmosphere was just perfect. The wind blew gently, and the trees smelt like fresh mint apples. I had barely run two hundred meters when I ran into him, and he was still as dashing as I remembered, with his calmly looking eyes and unevenly short combed hair. When he looked up and spotted me at the other end of the road, his eyes lit up like the stars that adorned the moon, and the corners of his lips turned up, forming a smile. I couldn't help it; I smiled back.

BLAKE

John and his friends were the life of the party. They had consumed a lot of alcohol even before the event had started, and they were practically drunk by the time we were doing shots.

The event started with a speech from the organizer, Angela Vasquez, who had been the high school valedictorian. There wasn't a real schedule of activities planned after Angela's speech. All we were told to do was volunteer to go up on stage and talk about the career paths we had followed after high school, say anything we'd ever wanted to say to anyone present, and maybe sing or do whatever we wanted to. Angela was a big-shot event planner who lived in New York, and I was really pleased for her. She looked happy and very different from the girl I'd taken to the prom. I gathered from John that he had become a carpenter and hadn't moved from Chicago. He hadn't attended college either. I suddenly looked at the group—John's friends—and it seemed as if they did this quite often. So, I asked each one of them if they had gone to college and what they were doing with their lives at the moment.

One was a plumber, the other said he owned his own hardware store, and the last was a mechanic. Not one of them had gone to college. They said that they went to Benjamin's every other day. Benjamin's was the most popular pub in the district. This was actually their routine. They were all doing commendable jobs, but I'm not sure if I wanted to be associated with them. They'd continued to hold the same views and ideologies over the last fifteen years; nothing had changed. They had also settled for the comfortable life; they had not pushed themselves the way I had. I suddenly felt weird being around them. I looked at them closely, and I could see their eyes saying it, even if their lips did not, and they thought it in their hearts: I had become a sell-out to them. I suddenly yearned for Seattle: to be in my wife's arms and kiss her lips again as we lay in our mightily comfortable bed. I wanted to lie in bed with her and nurse her back to health. I thought back to this morning. She hadn't even acknowledged my goodbye and hadn't let me kiss her. She'd said that she hadn't wanted me to get the flu, but I knew it was more than that.

She hadn't wanted me there; it was obvious that I repelled her. I checked my phone for any calls, but there were none. If she'd missed me or even thought about me, she would have called. I was about to put my phone back in my pocket and continue drinking with John and the gang when I heard her. The voice was all too familiar. It was Alice Kennedy, and she was on stage. I stared blankly at her, and the memories of the kiss flooded in torrentially. Every moment was ingrained in my memory: the shock on Ryan Green's face, the books in Angela Vazquez's hands, and Alice's shiny, cinnamon-flavored lip gloss and the soft texture of her lips.

"Hi! I'm Alice Kennedy. I'm a lawyer now, and I live in Cali." Everyone clapped at the end of her introduction. She had become more beautiful than I could have imagined, and she had a banging body, too. Yes, I was a married man, but she looked sexy in that red dress she wore. The crowd egged her on to say something to someone. She obliged after a little persistence.

"*Okay. Blake Adams, stop staring at me. It was just one kiss, and it was fifteen years ago.*" This is what I imagined she would say; but, instead, she said, "John Ridgewell, I know it's free beer, but if you don't stop, it seems you might soon go into labor with that fat belly." Everyone, including John, burst into laughter, and then our eyes met—mine and Alice Kennedy's. I held her gaze for a few seconds before she said, "I would like to sing *Endless Love* and dedicate it to everyone here and their lovers. May the love not depart from you." She then proceeded to sing it, and it was beautiful.

I saw her saunter toward me after her performance, hips swaying from side to side, hands clenched in each other, and then a large smile formed on her face.

"Alice Kennedy. The big-shot lawyer." I moved into her embrace, and she held on for some seconds longer than allowed.

"Blake Adams. How are you?"
"I've been normal . . . just living. If I didn't know any better, I'd think you dedicated that song, 'Endless Love,' to me."

"No. I dedicated it to John and his beer." We both laughed at this momentarily before she said, "So, tell me, what do you do? Are you married? Any kids?"

"I'm an architect, and I live in Seattle. I'm married to the most amazing woman on the planet. No kids. What about you?"

"I'm not married. Believe it or not, it's really hard to find good men in California. I was engaged once, but it didn't work out."

I was beginning to feel light-headed; the effect of the alcohol was starting to kick in. I intentionally ignored her downplaying how amazing her body was, because I knew this was just some reverse psychology. She would say things like "my thighs look a bit full" or "my stomach needs to be flatter". I would praise her body, and she would downplay it and then just make me praise it more so she could truly believe me. I wasn't falling for that. It was the oldest trick in the book.

I looked around, and John and his gang looked drab; they seemed exhausted from all the beer drinking . . . maybe even drunk. They seemed to be in a deep discussion with a particular group that looked equally drunk. Someone was on the stage singing a song that I had never heard before, and the rest of the crowd seemed engulfed in the performance; there really was no other option.

"Okay. Where do you want to go?"

"How about you wait and find out?" she asked with a sultry look in her eyes. She then grabbed me by the hand and dragged me towards the gymnasium's exit.

JENNIFER

I walked him to my house and when we arrived, I suggested to Bill to take a shower since he sweated a storm and smelled like an old sweaty sock. Luckily, Bill is the same size as Blake so he was able to wear a pair of Blake's old clothes and pair of shoes. We decided to catch up on the years that we had spent apart and shared memories of old. Bill and I had grown up together in Baltimore; we'd attended the same elementary school, middle school, and high school. He'd worked at an advertising agency like I had, and he now lived in San Francisco. He had moved away with his parents to San Francisco just after high school, and I hadn't seen him since. It was refreshing meeting someone from Baltimore—especially someone who knew most of the things about me that I had intentionally left in my past.

"You still haven't told me why you're in Seattle," I said as we both relaxed on the mini dining room table that Blake and I had just bought at a garage sale.

"Company convention. I'll be in town for three days," he said. He then added, "Your home is lovely."

I nodded in agreement, as if I had already known that he would have said this. I glanced at his finger and noticed there was no ring. "Thank you. You never got married?" I listened to myself, and I could tell how intrusive the question sounded, so I added, "You don't have to answer that."

"I'm divorced. I have a kid, though . . . Reginald. He's five." He proceeded to show me a couple pictures of Reginald on his phone. He was really adorable . . . just like his father at that age, and I unconsciously blurted this out. Bill rolled over in his chair laughing, and I felt my face flush with embarrassment.

"Remember that one time you got drunk and ended up making out with a mannequin?" We started to laugh together and speaking about forgotten memories and wild moments.

"Remember when you puked on Frank McKinnon and then apologized and then did it again?" Now, we were both reeling with laughter, and then he said, "Remember when we drove in Anderson's car and had that David Bowie song blaring through the speakers and then you raised your arms as high as you could in the back seat of the car with no seat belt and said 'In these rare moments of serendipity and wild adventures alone, do I feel alive!'?"

"Yes, I do. How come you remember that?" I was in awe at his recollection, but I remembered that day. It was the day Bill and I first made out. We took charge and I felt limitless. As my hands flailed around like stringy noodles, I felt like anything was possible. I felt as if I could dream anything and it would come to fruition. I felt as if I owned that day. I felt alive. I needed that feeling again. "We should do that again."

"Don't you think we're too old for that?" he queried.

"No, no. We're not," I said before running to get the keys to Blake's car. I then dragged him along, and we went for a stroll to feel alive yet again.

I needed this; I needed to feel alive again. My marriage was fun, and Blake was a really great guy, but lately, my life had become routine, and even Blake had settled into this routine. He told the same jokes, still made his dishes with a little more salt than required, and followed the same method of foreplay before we made love. He had also stopped doing the little things, such as taking notice and acknowledging anytime

I changed my hairstyle, sending me texts during the day, playing strangers whenever I met him in public, and getting me flowers for no reason. I admit that he had spoiled me over the years, but I had also done the same, and I had not toned it down after marriage. I still got him gifts randomly, sent him texts out of the blue, and even massaged him to sleep on his tired days. I needed to go on this "feel alive" adventure with Bill; I needed to do something out of the ordinary, live on the edge again, and feel alive again.

BLAKE

As we left the gymnasium, Alice and I agreed it would be best for us to change into something more comfy so we decided to head to our cars to pick up some spare clothes and quickly change. As we walked together, I couldn't stop thinking about that kiss and how great she looked. I think this energy proved to be excessive for Alice, and she was not shy to exert it openly. She collected a guitar from a street performer as we walked along some close knit streets and were suddenly amidst between some odd looking buildings. Alice sang a mixture of classic and pop songs to a small, attentive audience of passersby that soon escalated into a large adoring crowd.

She gave all the money she raised from her singing effort to the street performer, who became tearful and was full of joy. It was the most heartwarming thing I had seen in a while. She screamed her lungs out into the open any chance she got, and she noticed the little things, such as my boyishly grey hair and my awkwardly cute posture. She also laughed wholeheartedly at my corny jokes. These were things Jennifer used to notice and complement each other on before, but she no longer put in any effort. I resolved to not think about Jennifer tonight; she clearly was not thinking about me. I began to feed off Alice's energy; it was really contagious and made me feel good. Eventually, we sat on the bench at the park, exhausted, and then we talked.

"You know, I think of that kiss from fifteen years ago," Alice said.

"Yeah? What about it?" I tried to say this casually, as if it meant nothing. But she held my gaze for a minute; I think she saw through me. She knew I was lying: I had thought about the kiss, I had thought about doing it again, and she knew it. It was obvious from the smirk on her face that she knew.

"Nothing. It's nothing," she said.

"I should get going. It's been a long day," I said to diffuse the erotic tension that was building between us.

She came closer until her lips were an inch away from mine, and then she said, "We probably should. We wouldn't want the inevitable to happen." I rose and attempted to smoothen the creases of my pants before asking a question that I wanted to take back the minute the words reeled off my lips.

"Where are you staying?" I asked.

"The Best Western. I assume you're staying with your parents?"

I wanted to lie and say yes; I really should have, now that I think about it in retrospect. But instead, I said, "No. I'm staying at the Best Western, too."

"Really? Come on! I've got something to show you." She took one look at me and then took off. I ran closely behind her, and then I felt a smile curl my lips. I was happy. This was my first time being genuinely happy in weeks. I had missed that feeling. I charged toward her, and we ran in the direction of the Best Western, taking the energy of the day with us. We eventually ran out of breath and took a cab.

Her room was large and outlandish. It was not like my bland, regular room, which had just a bed, a TV, and a bathroom. I felt cramped in mine, but hers was spacious. She had a couch, a flat-screen TV, and a Jacuzzi. She was living the life. I started to wonder if she was really a lawyer or whether it was a front. She pointed me to the couch and went about searching for something in her luggage. She came back later with two large, white, cardboard-like materials rolled up like the scrolls used in ancient times. She rolled them open, and there lay before me were the most beautiful pieces of art I had ever seen. The first was a painting of the skyline of Chicago, and its detailing was amazing. It had all the sights I grew up adoring from the bell tower of our high school; she must have drawn it from there. It was breathtaking to behold, and as I continued to stare at it, it brought back once-forgotten memories. I remembered the nights I overheard my mom and dad yelling at each other; the times I saw my dad late at night with different ladies; the day my mom was in a hit-and-run accident, having gone looking for my dad, who was having one of his various trysts; and the feel of my mother's hand in mine at the hospital as she took her last breath. I blamed my father for her death, and I still had not forgiven him.

Throughout these difficult times, the things that had kept me sane had been the skyline and the bright lights from the bell tower, as well as the thought that one day, I would make something of myself, marry a girl my mother would be proud of, and be the father my father never was to my own kids.

Alice rolled the next painting open before saying, "I've got to go freshen up. I'll be back in a minute." I nodded to acknowledge that I had heard her. I didn't think the second painting was as exquisite as the first, particularly because I didn't have any personal connection to it, but it was an equally great work of art. It portrayed the famous Sunset Boulevard. I had never been to Los Angeles but it looked lifelike. Alice sashayed back into the room in a white bathrobe, water still dripping from her hair.

"These paintings are really good. Did you paint these?" I asked as she dried her hair with a towel.

"Yes, I did."

"You can sing, paint, and, from the looks of it, you're a badass lawyer, too. What *can't* you do?"

"Keep a man!" She laughed immediately. It was the same wholehearted, deep laughter that emanated when she spoke about her relational ties with men.

"You seem really happy without one, though," I said before averting my eyes from the bed, where she sat rubbing her legs with some sort of lotion. I didn't think she was doing it to seduce me; she wasn't even looking in my direction as she did it. She continued rubbing from her ankles up to her knees before moving slowly to her thighs. I refocused my gaze on the painting I held in my hands. It was the Chicago skyline from the bell tower.

"I'm giving them out to an art gallery downtown. They'll sell them to raise money for charity." She was still focused on her lotion-rubbing body exploration, although her hands were in a less sensual position than before. Alice slipped into some nice revealing pare of clothes and her natural beauty stopped me for a brief moment. Back to the painting, I thought it was noble of her to give these beautiful pieces to charity. I wanted the one of the Chicago skyline, but then I felt guilty depriving homeless people of money they needed.

"You seem intrigued by the painting of the skyline; do you want to take it?" She walked over and sat beside me on the couch. "I drew it from a picture I took from the bell tower at our school."

"I want it. I'm totally going to pay for it, and then you can give the money to charity."

She objected. "You don't have to. Take it as a gift from me to you."

I was speechless. She was extremely nice. I wondered what would have become of us if I had acted on that kiss from fifteen years ago. "Thank you." I moved in for a hug, and she hugged me more tightly than I expected, pressing her body against me for longer than was permitted for a married man and a single woman.

"I still think about the kiss from fifteen years ago, too." I hated myself for saying it, but I felt that it needed to be said. It made her loosen her grip on me and break out of the hug.

"Really?" I saw her eyes widen in amazement. She moved closer. The sides of our bodies rubbed against each other's. She rested her head against my shoulders, and then she said, "I should have acted on it, but I didn't think you liked me that way."

"I did. I was just scared it would ruin me if you didn't reciprocate my affection."

"Wait . . . you did?" she asked before looking up at me. Her beautiful eyes made me feel vulnerable; I felt as if she was seeing through me. We didn't speak for a few seconds; we just stared at each other, letting our eyes communicate our thoughts. She inched closer and leaned in to kiss me. I turned my face, and she kissed my cheek. We didn't speak; but, after a while, the awkwardness still didn't fade, so I spoke.

"I can't. I'm married."

"I know. But I also know you feel what I'm feeling."

"I have to go. I'm sorry for leading you on. I guess I just wanted to feel wanted again. I'm sorry." I arose from the couch, but she held me back.

"Don't go. I promise I won't make a move on you. I could use you here and need someone to talk to." She placed one hand on her chest and raised the other as if she were swearing in front of a jury. "I swear. I won't make a move. Just stay, for old times' sake."

"Okay." I sat back down. "For old times' sake."

JENNIFER

The ride was as exhilarating as I imagined it would be. Bill drove and played the same David Bowie song, while I sat in the back of the car and raised my arms as high as I could as if I was the freest person alive.

I felt sixteen again and as if I was back in Baltimore, where all that mattered to me were my books and music. I felt as if life was an unending continuum. I felt limitless again, but I wanted to feel this chapter six text here. Insert chapter six text here. Insert chapter six text way with his arms around me. I wanted to spend this moment with Blake. He was all I had been thinking about. I remembered our first kiss in his crappy old college apartment; I remembered him driving all the way down to Baltimore for my father's funeral, even though we weren't dating; and I remembered the very first gift he bought me—a vintage gold necklace—which I made him give back, and we used the money to pay his heating bill. He then bought me a similar gold necklace when he got his first paycheck after college.

I remembered when we moved in together, and the way he beamed with smiles when I got us matching bracelets, and I remembered the day he asked me to marry him; he had planned it for weeks. Wanting it to be just perfect, he took me to the rooftop of the Three Taverns, our favorite hangout spot in the city, and then we watched the city lights, discussing where we wanted to be in five years' time. I told him that I hoped to be the senior vice president at the advertising agency where I worked, probably be engaged, to travel the world, and then see where life took me. Then, I asked him, "Where would you like to be in the next five years?" and he said "With you . . . being married to you." He knelt on one knee and brought out a diamond ring. "Jennifer Violet Lancaster," and as he said these words, the tears welled up in my eyes, "will you marry me?"

"Yes. Yes. Yes!" I said, as I reveled in uncontainable excitement. I felt a raindrop on my nose, and in less than a minute, it became a torrential downpour, and we just laughed because this was Seattle, the home of rain. Despite his weeks of careful planning, it had rained on our parade. We didn't quiver or run for shelter; we stayed in the rain and basked in the moment. He called someone, and we watched as fireworks decorated the sky; it was beautiful. I missed him. I yearned for him as the winds blew across my face. I needed my husband back.

After we drove past the tunnel, I asked Bill to stop the car, and then I got out of the car from the back and told him to switch to the passenger seat. I had owned our moment, and now, I was going home. Bill was filled with excitement when we got back. He said that he hadn't done something that out of the blue in decades. We sat at the table and chatted over wine.

"Did you hear about Frank?" he asked.

"What about him?"

"He's in jail. Grand larceny." He said this casually, as if it was the expected outcome for someone like Frank, and if I was being honest, I was not exactly surprised. Frank had been involved in so many illegal activities back in high school.
"Wow. I feel so bad. You know I didn't call him after prom."
"I know. He told me." Bill says this and then stares at me awkwardly for a few minutes

"What?" I retorted.

"You haven't changed since high school—still as beautiful as I remember." I found myself blushing at this; it was a little weird. I knew I was beautiful; it just felt refreshing hearing it from someone other than Blake, although I would have liked to hear Blake say it more often. Bill got our glasses and then took them to the kitchen; he was really a gentleman.

"Why did you get divorced, Bill?" I knew it sounded a little intrusive, but I wanted to know if that was where Blake and I were headed.

He looked me dead in the eye and said, "I was a bad husband. She really did more than enough as a wife." He seemed to be telling the truth, and I felt pity for him. "I cheated, Jen. I screwed up. Men cheat a lot these days; you've got someone special in Blake. Don't screw it up." I walked over and hugged him, as I felt he needed it.

BLAKE

I exited arrivals at the airport and saw her waiting there for me. She held a placard that read "Mr. Pierre Dupont." Pierre Dupont was my French alter ego, and I used the name whenever we were role-playing. Pierre is a French businessman who goes on holiday to Mexico and falls in love with a Mexican barista named Rosario Lopez. But their love is opposed my Rosario's father, who has betrothed her to the son of a wealthy Mexican. Together, Pierre and Rosario elope to France, where they live happily ever after. This was the storyline of our last role-playing adventure. We usually spun the story into different unscripted fantasies of our choosing, but one thing was certain—the names of the characters remained unchanged.

She ran into my embrace, and I hugged her tightly.

She smelled like a fresh bouquet of sunflowers . . . or maybe it was the flashy red dress she wore that made me feel this way. On the way home, I told her about John Ridgewell, his pot belly, and his incessant drinking. I told her about how drab the reunion was and how she had dodged a bullet by not being there. I also told her about Alice's painting and her singing, carefully omitting my visit to her room; I knew that she would freak out if I told her that part.

When we got home, I unpacked my bags and showed her Alice's painting. We both took a few minutes to fully appreciate the masterpiece. We didn't speak; we just stared at it, taking it all in. I presented her with some earrings I'd gotten for her in Chicago, and she gushed at them, but I refused to tell her that Alice had helped pick them out. She then told me about Bill and how she had run into him during her occasional run.

"We totally owned that day," she said. "We went for a drive, then I was in the back of the car like good old times, feeling free and alive while we had David Bowie playing on the stereo. It was magical." She was trying to put on the new earrings using the bedroom mirror.

I wanted to say that she could always feel that way with me but I didn't. I knew this might cause friction between us again, as she would think I was trying to compete with Bill and replace what they once shared together. Besides, I just wanted to enjoy our renewed connection, so instead, I asked, "I thought you were seriously down with the flu? How were you able to do all this? Weren't you meant to be in bed resting?"

JENNIFER

"I thought you were seriously down with the flu? How were you able to do all this? Weren't you meant to be in bed resting?"

As soon as I heard these words, I started panicking. Just to avoid an argument, I mumbled something inaudible—I told him I was going to get some juice—and then I left the room. I knew that if I said that I had decided not to go to the reunion, after promising that I would, just because I didn't feel like it, we would have an argument that would ripple into the other minor arguments that we had been avoiding for weeks.

Downstairs, the house looked different, felt different, and smelled different. It was like I was seeing it through someone else's eyes and this was my first time in my own house. I walked to the fridge to get juice before I realized what was different; it was him. He smelled different, and he acted different, especially when I tried to evade the argument with some flimsy mumbled jargon. Something was wrong, and I needed to figure it out.

I walked back up the stairs. He had gone into the bathroom. I could hear the water running; he was in the shower. I looked around, spotted his phone on the bedside table, scurried over, and unlocked it. I glanced through the pictures of the night before, and a stocky, pot-bellied white man appeared in many of them. He was always holding a bottle of beer in his hand, and I assumed that he was John Ridgewell.

Just as I was scrolling through, Blake received an MMS message; it was from a lady named Alice. The picture featured her laying her head on Blake's shoulder while he held a painting in his hands. They were

29

both beaming with smiles. Alice had written: "We should do this again if you are ever in Los Angeles. We could go see Sunset Boulevard." I felt the anger raging in me, but I also felt weak. I wanted to cry, but I would not give him the pleasure of seeing me vulnerable; he didn't deserve it. I awaited his exit from the bathroom while I wondered how and where we had gone wrong in our marriage. How could he cheat on me? How? No wonder he hadn't flinched nor offered to nurse me back to wellness when I'd said I was down with the flu. I heard the shower turn off and the water stop running. He came out with a lopsided grin on his face, towel hanging loosely around his waist. He moved in for a kiss, but I pushed him back with my hand and asked, "Why? Why are you cheating on me, Blake?"

BLAKE

I came out of the shower, and there she was. My woman. My heart. My love. She looked as sexy as could be in her tightly fitted outfit which made her natural beauties standout. I thought back to Chicago and reaffirmed to myself that I had made the right decision with Alice. I had decided to stay faithful, and it felt good. Jennifer had done nothing to warrant me cheating on her, and I loved her deeply. I could not have thrown this all away just because of my first ever kiss and the need to feel that way again . . . not when I actually knew that feeling of naiveté could be experienced only once in a lifetime. I felt bad that I had even considered it at all.

I moved in for a kiss, but she pushed me away. I was confused. Had I done something wrong? Was it because I had chosen to ignore her mumblings when I had asked her about the flu? She stared me down for at least a minute before asking, "Why? Why are you cheating on me, Blake?" I was surprised and equally confused, so I stuttered for a couple seconds because I really didn't know what to say.

"I am not cheating on you, Jen! Why would I?"

"You don't have to lie anymore. Tell me . . . what does she really offer you? "

Her tears were welling up now, but I could see clearly that she was trying to hold them back. "Name it, Blake, and I would do it for you. I could get plastic surgery if you want! Just freaking tell me!" She flashed my phone across my face, and I snatched it from her hands. It was a picture of Alice and me, and in it, her head lay on my chest while I held the Chicago skyline in my hands.

"Jen, listen to me!" I held her shoulders, but she shrugged them away.

"I'm sorry I didn't mention Alice. I really didn't mention her because I figured this was how you would react." She scoffed at this. "Alice and I went to the same high school, and she was first girl I ever kissed. We ran into each other at the reunion. Nothing happened. We just hung out after, and then she offered to show me her paintings, and I obliged. Nothing happened, Jen. But this would not have happened if you'd just come with me to the reunion, instead of pretending to be down with the flu."

"SO, YOU ARE BLAMING THIS ON ME NOW?"

She was screaming now, but I tried to keep my voice calm. "I am not. I'm just saying you should have come."

"IT IS YOUR FAULT I PRETENDED TO BE DOWN WITH THE FLU! YOU WERE NOT PUTTING IN ANY EFFORT!"

"My fault? PARDON ME FOR BEING THE BEST HUSBAND I COULD POSSIBLY BE!"

I was screaming now, but I really didn't want to. So, I sighed and then dressed up before storming out of the room. I picked up the keys and left the front door banging in my wake.

Thirty minutes later, I was at Vince's house. Vince and I had gone to college together and had been roommates from sophomore year till I'd gotten engaged. He was also married and had no kids. Vince cheated on his wife, and he blamed her for it. She had started cheating on him first. I knew that he was essentially not the best person to consult for marital advice, but I was really out of options. He was the only one who understood the relationship between Jennifer and me.

Vine was watching a basketball game, with a beer in hand, when I walked in.

"Amazing that you didn't hear me knocking," I said.

"Such a gracious way to announce a return from Chicago. You always outdo yourself, Andrews."

I was still filled with anger, so I ignored his tart remark. "It's Jennifer, man. She's just driving me crazy"

He continued watching the basketball game without even glancing my way. It was almost as if I were nonexistent. He then took a chug of beer before saying, "Hey, I know you guys don't usually have problems. I'm sure you'll sort it out. You know what to do. Jen is a real gem." He took another swig of beer. "Make sure you don't lose her."

I took a deep breath, and it hit me. I really knew what to do; Alice and the flu were not really worth fighting over. I spent another five minutes watching the game with Vince. "Good talk, Vince," I said before leaving his place.

I texted Jen on my way home from Vince's place: "Rosario, these forces are trying to separate us, but I won't let them. I still love you."

She replied a minute later: "Come home, Pierre. I miss you."

Immediately after I parked the car in the garage, I looked over her text for a minute. I then walked into the house, and then she ran to me. I grabbed her and pinned her to the nearest wall, kissing her passionately. We made love, and it was special. It felt brand new . . . as if it was my first time with her.

Afterward, she laid her head on my chest, and then I said, "I am sorry about the Alice thing. I really should have told you regardless of my apprehensions."

She raised her head toward me and looked at me. "I'm sorry for lying about the flu and for being such a grouch these past few weeks. You really didn't deserve it."

"I really don't deserve someone like you. You're more than amazing."

"No. No. No." She sat upright and cupped my face in her hands. "You're the best husband anyone could ever have, and there's no one more deserving of me than you."

I nodded in affirmation and then smiled to myself. *This reverse psychology thing really does work.*

JENNIFER

Last night, I slept off while lying on his chest after passionate love making. I heard a voice saying things in the growing distance, but I ignored it. It persisted until I felt a nudge on my shoulder, and then the voice became clearer. It was Blake. He whispered, "Awaken, my love."

Groggily, I arose. "What time is it?"

"It's a little after ten in the morning, my love."

I saw a tray of scrambled eggs set carefully with sausage and steak, and a cup of tea had been placed by the side. "Wow," I gasped. He then brought a bouquet of flowers from behind him, and I really became speechless; he hadn't done this in a long while.

"You deserve this and so much more, my princess," he said.

I was actually tearing up, and this made it very hard for me to speak, but I wanted to tell him how amazing he was and how I really was the one who was undeserving of him . . . that he was too good for me.

He continued, "I should have stayed with you and offered to nurse you to health when you were down with the flu. I'm sorry, and even though I haven't said it often lately, I still think you're the most beautiful woman I've ever seen."

"Really?"

"Yes." He said this with a lost puppy look, and it was the most adorable thing I had seen in weeks, so I leaned in and kissed him deeply.

"I promise to be a better wife to you."

"I promise to be a better husband to you," he replied, finally realizing that we made a great team and were a perfect hubby and wife duo.

I see a wry smile form at the corner of his lips, and then he whisper-says, "I am so lucky to have you in my life."

We were super excited about our relationship and commitment to one another like an old married couple. We felt inseparable and hugged each other tightly.

ABOUT THE AUTHOR

My passion to create began as a child. I remember spending long nights at a friend's house writing random stories in the hope that one day my stories would come to life and readers would be touched by them.

I have so many stories to tell and I am really excited to share them with you. I would love for you "the reader" to have a great experience with the unique style of short stories presented to you.

www.ingramcontent.com/pod-product-compliance
Lightning Source LLC
Chambersburg PA
CBHW020606130626
46552CB00007B/3073